# Winter adventures
## (a Novel)

By:

Raykhona Norova

© Taemeer Publications LLC
**Winter adventures**
by: Raykhona Norova
Edition: August '2023
Publisher:
*Taemeer Publications LLC* (Michigan, USA / Hyderabad, India)

© Taemeer Publications

| | | |
|---|---|---|
| Book | : | ***Winter adventures*** |
| Author | : | Raykhona Norova |
| Publisher | : | Taemeer Publications |
| Year | : | '2023 |
| Pages | : | 42 |
| Title Design | : | *Taemeer Web Design* |

## Chapter 1

*Meet your friend Charlie*

Charlie is your friend who lives in the stormy north. Charlie's father died of an illness when he was one year old. Charlie, who was raised by his widowed mother at the age of one, did not feel his father's love all his life. All of this started on the twenty-fourth of November. As it is very cold outside, the house is warmed only by the burning fireplace. Early in the morning, his mother would come to collect firewood after breakfast, and Charlie would not leave the house and wait for his mother to come. Charlie sat down. Then Charlie, who was bored, went out into the street. There is no storm on the street, the snowstorm is the reason for playing. Charlie played snowstorm for ten minutes and got bored and didn't know what to do. A minute later, a sound like howling was heard from the snow-covered forest near the hut. Intelligent Charlie immediately recognized that it was the sound of a depressed wild dog.

## Chapter 2

### *A great friend*

Charlie walked slowly to a one-month-old puppy in the woods, shivering from hunger and cold. Charlie felt so sorry for the puppy that he wished he could do something to help him. Then Charlie had an idea. He slowly took the puppy in his arms to the hut in front of him. He entered the house and gave the puppy a piece of bread. The dog was scared first and then slowly started sniffing. When he realized that there is no danger here, he started to feel tired. At that moment, his mother, whose face was red from the cold, came in carrying a bundle of firewood. Mrs. Lily, who opened her mouth in surprise, was stunned for a while, and then began to question Charlie in a panic;

- Did you go near the forest, Charlie?!

Lady Lily's angry eyes were only on Charlie.

- After all, he was helpless!, - whispered Charlie.

- Turn off your voice! How many times have I told you not to go near the forest, - cried Mrs. Lily.

- He called me for help! "Should I have watched him die," explained Charlie.

- It's good, - said Mrs. Lily. But now take it to its place.

- He will die there. Look, it's very small. Please let him stay with us, - asked Charlie.

- After all, Charlie - Mrs. Lily suddenly relaxed before she could finish her sentence.

- Oh, - continued Charlie crushed. Let him be my best friend.

- It's good, - Mrs. Lily said, blessing our family!

"AWESOME!" Charlie shouted. Mom, what shall we name him?- said Charlie.

- It's better to name him Alpha, - suggested Mrs. Lily.

- Nice name! Charlie cheered.

- Alpha, now you will be our guard, - said Mrs. Lily cheerfully.

## Chapter 3

### *Unhappy days*

Alpha was becoming more and more powerful and beautiful. Alpha really became a faithful guardian of this family, and a kind friend to Charlie. In the small village, everyone loved Alfa and called him "Village Guardian". This name is certainly not in vain. One day, when everyone was sleeping, a wolf came to the village. Then Alpha woke up everyone with a loud howl and people chased the wolf away. He told us in advance that there would be an avalanche the other day. So, in a word, Alfa was liked by everyone. But Charlie's mother decided to go on a trip one day.

- Charlie, they are calling me to work in the south. If our work goes well, we will get rid of this village and our dilapidated hut.

- Take me too, honey.

- Don't be afraid, my child, Aunt Pipi will stay with you.

- No, mom. I will live alone with Alfa until you come.

- Don't say that, Charlie, your Aunt Pippi is very kind. Your aunt will take care of you until I return.

- Charlie, is everything okay?

- Okay, but hurry up. I don't get along very well with Aunt Pippi.

- That's it, cheer up! Now go to sleep. In the morning you have breakfast with your Aunt Pippi.

## Chapter 4

*Aunt Pippi*

When Charlie got up in the morning, his mother was already gone and Aunt Pippi was preparing breakfast.

- Hello, Aunt Pippi, good morning.

- Hello Charlie, good morning to you too.

- Has my mother already left?

- Yes, more than three hours, my dear! As you say yes, come and collect firewood with Alfa from the forest. Soon the fireplace will go out. The house is also very cold.

- Good, Aunt Pippi (Charlie later learns that Aunt Pippi's real name is Petunia).

Charlie became fluent in collecting firewood with Alpha. But he did not yet know that a great danger awaited him. Charlie, who went into the forest after gathering firewood, was startled by the rustling of something. It was some kind of gigantic animal. Charlie took a bag of firewood and started to run away with Alpha. Fortunately, the animal did not chase after them. Charlie and Alpha left the forest and went to the hut.

- Oh, dear, give me the firewood. My dear, your dog is very smart.

-"Yes," said Charlie happily.

- Give this to Alfa and then sit down to eat. I'm going to put some fire in the fireplace until then. Shall we come Charlie?!

After finishing her speech, Aunt Pipi handed Alpha a piece of chicken meat and two pieces of bread. Alpha, who was happy with the food given by Charlie, hurriedly devoured his share. Meanwhile, Charlie himself sat down at the table.

- Aunt Pippi - asked Charlie.

- I'm so cute - Aunt Pippi faked a smile.

"Mom, when will she come?" Charlie asked sadly.

- My dear, your mother said that if she works for six months, they will give her a house from the south. Then, as long as you don't live here, in your cold, dilapidated huts - said Aunt Pippi with a sly smile.

- This means that I have been living here with you for half a year, Aunt Pipi.

- Yes, my dear - Aunt Pippi whispered incredulously.

Then Charlie made up his mind that tonight he would sneak away from Aunt Pippi and go south to find his mother.

## Chapter 5

*The Trip*

In the evening, Charlie waited for Aunt Pippi to fall asleep, took food and water and went on the road with Alpha. But this trip was very dangerous. And the compass always shows the south where it is crooked. On top of that, he is about to run out of food. Alpha is also hungry. The last time he walked that far was when he ate a dead fox a week ago. But he still has to walk to the south during the month. Food is scarce, and Charlie and Alpha are starving. Even if he goes back now, he will die even if he goes forward.

- That's it, Alpha, there's not much left to do - thought Charlie.

Then suddenly Charlie's vision became blurry.

- BOOMING!!!

Charlie lost his strength and fell to the ground with a heavy blow. Alpha howled in agony, there is no way out. They lay like that until night. Now Alpha is exhausted. He stopped howling and lay down next to the Charlie. Charlie is still breathing but very slowly. If he sleeps like this from evening to morning, he will surely die of cold. The last link. If no one comes to help now, both Alpha and Charlie will disappear from this world. In general, it is clear that they will die. So anyone can be in these rare places. If Charlie hadn't set off on his own, who knows if he would have been sleeping sweetly with Aunt Pippi in front of the fireplace in his cozy cabin. Alpha and Charlie fell asleep. Alpha woke up in the morning. He looks at some house. Charlie is also lying on the bed in the room. No, the true Alpha is not dreaming. It seems that someone saw them and brought them home. Yes, that's exactly what happened. I wonder who brought them here. Very interesting. Then the door opened and a Hindu came in. He had enough food for Charlie and Alpha. He said something to his friend in a language Alpha did not understand. Then Charlie woke up. At the beginning, he was in a daze, like Alpha, and then he came back to his senses. Hindoo calmed Charlie down and left. Charlie and Alpha ate enough.

- What do you say Alpha, how did they find us - asked Charlie. But Alpha's ears and eyes were now on the pork meat. Knowing this, Charlie turned it off.

Later, that Indian led another man and sat down in front of Charlie. In fact, the person in front of the Hindu seems to be a translator, and whatever the Hindu says, that person delivers his English to Charlie.

- Hey, boy, where did you come from and how did you get here? - asked the translator.

- I went to the south looking for my mom- answered Charlie.

- After all, the south is still very far! Where did you go from? - the translator asked Charlie with surprise.

- Yes, very long - said Charlie. I left for the road from the north and I passed out after I ran out of food - Charlie explained.

- Good - the translator nodded. We can help you.

-"Really," said Charlie.

- Yes, it's true. But you should be our guest until the end of winter. You can't go on a trip in winter, kid.

- But there are still less than two months until the end of winter!

- Right boy. If you want, you can go out now and die halfway, do you want that?

- Of course not.

- So our door is always open for you. Or rather, you and your dog.

- Good, sir.

- Very quiet little one. So what's your name?

- Charlie, Sir.

- It is a very beautiful name. So when do you start work?

- Wow, what kind of work, sir?

- You protect our hands with your dog. Can you do it?

- Yes, sir.

- Then get to work.

- Good, sir.

# Chapter 6

## *In a Hindu family*

Charlie and Alpha immediately went to work. At the beginning, they had a hard time keeping sheep, but later it became easy for them. Days went by. In the meantime, Charlie learned the Indian language and was able to speak it fluently. One day Charlie and Indian Kluch had a conversation that went something like this:

- Charlie, sit next to me for a minute. We need to discuss a couple of things.

- Good. What sir?

- Charlie, I hope you understand what I'm saying.

- Sir, I don't understand what you mean.

- That's all, listen to it. Since you came, that is, since Alfa came, my income has increased a lot. Soon winter will end and spring will come.....and....and.

- And I'm going south.

- Yes, you will go, Alfa will also go. Since the arrival of Alpha, the sheep have stopped disappearing by themselves. That is, I mean...

- That is, you want to buy Alfa.

- Yes. Likewise.

- Are you kidding me sir?

- No, Charlie.

- I will not sell Alfa, sir.

- I will give you how many millions you ask. So, how much do you ask?

- Sir, I told you, I will say it again, I WILL NOT SELL ALPHA!

- CHARLIE!

- I thought you were a good person, sir.

- Charlie where are you going?

- Go to the open grave.

- Don't overdo it Charlie Hadding!

- You have increased, sir! Know that a friend cannot be sold for money. I WILL NOT SELL ALPHA, UNDERSTAND.

- CHARLIE!!!

Charlie gathered everything he had and bought bread and meat with the money he had lost so far and went south with Alfa.

The road is very long and dangerous, but nothing can stop Charlie now. Only if there is Alfa next to him. Aunt Pippi and Kluch don't matter to Charlie anymore. Charlie is ready for anything now that he has his mother and Alpha.

- Alpha, I tortured you too - asked Charlie.

- Alpha nodded in response.

There is still a long way to go, and our bread is not enough. Okay Alpha, one death for one head, we must move forward no matter what. Alpha, we will have to spend the night here today.

Charlie, who was sleeping in the evenings with burning eyes, realized that the wolves had been following him for several days. The wolves seem to know the smell of Charlie's food. But the wolves are not going to give up on Charlie. There is no strength for that. They just want to eat Charlie's food. Then, like a light bulb, Charlie had a brilliant idea. Even if it didn't help, Charlie decided to train the wolves and get to the south quickly by sledding. Charli gave bread little by little and gathered the wolves around him. There are not many wolves, only three.

- Well, that's it. These are not wolves but oh my God, they are stray dogs!!! They even have sledge marks on them.

Charlie immediately built a small but sturdy sled out of branches.

- Great - said Charlie, who finished the work.

Now the last step is to tie the dogs with a thread. Charlie got to work pulling out the yarn he had always kept with him from Kluch.

## Chapter 7

### *Another new journey*

-This is a wonderful sleigh - Charlie was happy. Now our path is much closer, Alfa.

They set off, but the dogs barked a lot.

The sled broke down halfway. It took a long time to prepare the sledge again. There are too many dogs and not enough food. Even now, Charlie has washed the branches, boiled them in a little water, and made them suitable for his dogs to chew on. Charlie had to eat the food he had prepared for his dogs because he didn't even have a single piece of bread left to eat. In any case, it's better to eat than not. Charlie and his dogs are alive because of this food. A week has passed since the beginning of the famine. For a week now, they have been eating the cooked branches. You can't help but admire that Charlie will not stop until he achieves his goal. Charlie is trying not to save his life, but to save the lives of his dogs, and he is not giving up. His dog's legs were also tired, and when he ran away from the wolf today, Alpha's leg was badly beaten. Alpha has been unable to walk for two days. It is difficult to find food on it. To fix the alpha's leg, you just need to poke the crow's brain. Otherwise, Alpha's leg will be lame for life. Charlie doesn't have a gun at all.

- Alpha, forgive me for putting you in a difficult situation.

-"No," Alpha nodded as if to say Charlie.

- Good! Alpha is very good. Wow, we have come a long way since we started. I think it is close to the south. Just hold on a little longer, Alpha. Is everything ok? Yes, Alpha. Please Alpha ……. Please …… - Charlie began to sob at this moment. Please Alpha let's fight for each other now. Surrender... Oh my God, it's my fault. It happened because of my arbitrariness and curiosity. It's my fault Alpha. Me. Me. And again I'm to blame Alpha.

- BOOMING...

- MY GOD, WHAT HAPPENED! Alpha, we are stuck on a big ice. Now we must move as slowly as possible. Yes, yes, this is very good. No, a piece of ice broke. Oh, sorry, what was it! Yes, Alpha is a dead crow! OF COURSE IT IS!!! SAME!!! It's great, look at how good luck smiled at us, Alpha! Now your leg will definitely heal - he said, taking the crow from the water and pushing it on the leg of Alpha. He cleaned himself of feathers, minced meat and gave a spoonful to each dog. Although he had only half a spoonful of cereal left, Charlie, who was happy to feed his dogs, felt as if he had eaten a plate of cereal. It took Alfa a week for his leg to get better.

One day, Charlie found a tattered empty bed on the road. And in the evenings, he built a smaller tent for himself. In any case, the air is getting colder, which is a sign that it is on its way to the south.

Who knows, maybe Aunt Pippi panicked about Charlie's disappearance and alarmed Mrs. Lily.

- I think we will soon go to the south and see my mom, isn't it, Alpha?

- Woof, woof, woof- said Alpha.

- Well, if you join the sled from today, we could reach the south faster! It seems that your leg has become much better?

- Great food for breakfast today, my dears!

Charlie spread the rabbit meat he had recently bought on one of his dogs and shared it with everyone, including himself.

## Chapter 8

### *Road to the south*

- What do you think, Alpha, we are seeing a lot of dead birds recently. We have not known what hunger is for a long time. Maybe this is the blessing of nature to us. What do you think, Alpha?

- Woof, woof, woof

- Well then, let's get going as soon as possible. Now every second is precious for us, Alpha.

So Charlie is walking again. He walks, walks, even if he walks, he walks a lot. But this forest seems endless.

Charlie remembered his mother's advice that places closer to the south start to warm in the spring. One day, such conversations took place between mother and child:

Charlie: Mom, how do you know it's so close to south?

Mrs. Lily: Because, my son, in places near the south, intermittent heat begins in the spring.

Charlie: So, if the weather warms up, it will be close to the south.

Mrs. Lily: Yes, cute just like that, my smart, fluffy Charlie!

- That's why Charlie is not giving up. That is, he believes that he will reach the south.I like it. After the endless lands, a city appeared. Charlie, who was happy to see this, ran very fast towards the city. Yes indeed it is the biggest city in the south. Therefore, his mother is also in this city. When they entered the city, they thanked Charlie for feeding them so far without allowing the dogs to enter, and walked towards a small forest near the city. There is only Alpha in front of Charlie. Now Charlie needs only one thing to find his mom. But how? How will he find his mother in such a big city? If someone says that he will call his mom using his mobile phone, he will not know the number of his mom by heart. He is confused about what to do. Charlie kept walking towards the center of the city. Charlie, who had 3-4 thousand money in his hand, took one pie from a small shop in the city and ate half of it for Alfa and half of it himself. But how did he find his mom now? When Charlie was walking around the city, he saw an advertisement on a billboard and his eyes burst with joy.

ANNOUNCEMENT

THREE DOG COMPETITION!!!

We need three dogs who are smart, strong and brave in every way. It is better if the dogs have been on trips. If you have such a dog, go to the address below! The winning dog has two million prizes!!!

Address: Little Uingil town, District 66.

Good luck!!!

# PART 2

## Chapter 1

*New life*

After all, this is great news, Alpha. Two million-a. How wonderful is that! If you don't mind Alpha, I'll take you to this address. You're the best dog I've ever seen, aren't you?
Hearing that he was being praised, Alfa did his most sincere actions in this regard. Alpha and Charlie went to the address indicated in the advertisement. When they arrived at the address, they were greeted by a very handsome young man who was always smiling. And immediately informed his boss. The chief asked the following questions:
- Hello, young man. What is your name?
- Hello sir. My name is Corlin Charlie Sir.
- It is a very beautiful name. So what can your dog do?
- My dog is very smart. He will do whatever you say. And he can pass through various obstacles without difficulty.
- It's about such a guy. You will come to the exam early this week on Tuesday. There will be many dogs there. The total number of dogs is two hundred and thirteen. Only three of them will be selected. So, I got it, Mr. Corlin.
- Yes sir. Understandable.
- Very good. See you tomorrow then!
As Charlie left the room, he felt a strange feeling that he did not understand, neither joy nor fear. The most important thing is that he was able to reach the south safely. Nothing can attract him now except the principle of qualifying. Naturally, this feeling is also clearly felt in Alpha.

## Chapter 2

*Sorting principle*

The day Alpha and Charlie have been waiting for is finally here. They were met by the sir who spoke that day.

- Oh, and finally Mr. Corlin!

- Alfazar, there were two hundred and thirteen. We can start with the principle of sorting.

- Good Mr. Wright.

- Then check the microphone, Alfazar. I will start my speech.

- The microphone is ready for you, Mr. Wright.

- Then we started!

So - Mr. Wright started talking, as we are gathered in this place, I announce that the principle of selection has begun!!!

There was thunderous applause. Charlie was the last to finish clapping.

- After explaining the condition, three dogs that were able to cross this obstacle and stand up from the ball of fire without burning their hair, without being beaten or falling down will be accepted as candidates for the competition. If everyone is ready, WE START!!!

The dogs passed through the obstacles one after another. Charlie was the eighty-eighth. Out of eighty-seven dogs, only one was accepted as a competition candidate. And finally it was Charlie's dog Alpha's turn.

- Mister Corlin Charlie! - announced Sir Wright with pleasure.

- Oh, my God, Alpha, please carefully pass through the ring of fire. He is a very small ball.

- Faster - ordered Mr. Wright.

- Yes, now. Good luck, Alpha!

Maybe now the life and death of Alpha and Charlie is being decided, but literally, how their future will be is being decided.

Alfa has never given a warning in such obstacles. But how does it pass through the ring of fire? What about Alpha? Apparently, it is not difficult to understand that the feeling of fear is in Charlie, who is participating in the game.

- Keep it up, keep it up Alpha, you're great, YOU'RE GREAT!!! - Charlie was going to scream at least.

- Yes, yes, that's it, WONDERFUL - shouted Sir Wright.

- Yes, Alpha managed to pass through the ring of fire without falling or getting burned. You are great Alpha, you are the best!!! - Charlie hugged Alpha.

Half an hour later, the third claimant was also appointed.

There was no one left in the big hall except for the owners of the three contending dogs.

Mr. Wright went to congratulate everyone. Then to Charlie:

- As your dog is extremely fast, the boy left everyone speechless.

- Let's get back to the goal, that is, when and how the first competition will be.

- Then Mr. Wright gave a lecture about the "Three-Dog Competition", which has been organized for ten years.

"Good," began Mr. Wright cheerfully. The first competition will be held on the 18th of April, that is, ten days later. Since it is late today, I will explain the conditions of the first competition tomorrow at 9:00 in the morning. Is it ok?

- Yes, it is ok - everyone said

- Then it's good. Let's all go home, is it enough?

- Of course, they agreed.

And so Mr. Wright left the hall.

## Chapter 3

### *The first competition condition*

Charlie was so tired that day that instead of building his tent, he fell asleep on top of it.

The next day, he went to the big hall where the selection process took place. As always, Charlie and Alpha were greeted by Mr. Wright:

- Yes, my dears, I thought you would not come. Welcome!

- Thank you Mr. Wright.

- In that case, I can start explaining now. In the first competition, there will be very large fire obstacles, each of which has its own characteristics. At the end, there will be a ring of fire. That's all there is to it. Yes, by the way, my dears, we are trying to prevent your dog's fur from burning as much as possible. However, if the person hits the barrier and falls, the risk of death is high.

- WHAT? - asked all three applicants in unison.

- Yes, gentlemen, calm down a bit!

- After all, you didn't tell us this in advance, Sir Wright! Charlie asked excitedly.

- Mister Corlin, we are trying to reduce the risk of death as much as possible! In the previous ten years, these games did not end without death, Mr. Corlin Charlie!

After that, Mr. Wright gave a lecture about the games of the past years.

There are only five days left until the start of the first competition. But there are no conditions to prepare Alpha. Once or twice they asked Sir Wright for permission to prepare in the big hall. But he could not get permission. After that, Charlie thought that now Alpha just needs peace. Consequently, he also experienced difficult times. And so it is necessary to help Alpha to rest and gather strength. Alpha can do everything, he is a strong dog.

It seems that as the days are getting shorter, this kind of fear is appearing in Charlie;

With five days to go: Alpha will do everything, with two days to go: God, let everything end well, with one day to go: Oh God, save Alpha yourself, fears are clearly felt in Charlie. Alpha, on the contrary, the faster the days decrease, the faster his power increases. Yes, Alpha can control himself. He is facing the future without fear of anything. And this is good.

## Chapter 4

### *The first competition*

- Hello ladies and Gentlemen! Welcome to the Three Dog Competition! Let me explain the selection criteria. Our competition is completely different from other competitions. In our current conditions, two dogs that passed the first stage with excellent quality are considered to have passed to the second stage. One of our dogs, who passed the second condition perfectly, will pass the third stage on his own. A dog that can meet the third condition will be worth two million. If he can't pass, he will be chased away shamefully.

- Disgruntled shouts rang out in the great hall.

- There is no objection, my dears! Okay, now without grudge, I DECLARE the first condition OPEN!!!

- There was shouting and applause in the big hall.

Then the contending dogs went on stage and started the competition.

- Alpha, go ahead, Alpha, I trust you. You can do it all, trust me. You are the fiercest and bravest dog I have ever seen. Alpha, you are the only one, my love. You are one of the best dogs in the world. You are the only one! Such obstacles are not difficult for you. You have tried many of these in practice. Go ahead Alpha, good luck to you!!!

It seems that Charlie's words had a strong impact on Alpha, and Alpha's enthusiasm suddenly increased.

From somewhere came Sir Wright's shouts:

- Yes, one more obstacle and Corlin Alpha came first to the finish line! Alexander Alisia came second!!!

- Yes, yes, great Alpha! Charlie shouted.

- Alpha and Alicia passed to the second stage - announced Sir Wright.

After returning from the race, Charlie treated Alpha with ice cream. Alfa was very happy about this. Did he spend less effort for the competition? Charlie did not even notice that he fell asleep hugging Alpha.

The next day they prepared for the second competition. In any case, now Alpha's self-confidence is increasing. A person who sees Alpha on the street immediately takes a picture with him.

Yes, now the lives of Charlie and Alpha have changed radically. Now Charlie is writing a book about what is happening in his life. After all, nothing like that happened to a twelve-year-old boy. At the same time, Charlie is earning money by writing short stories. Both of them are full. In his spare time, Charlie wanders the city looking for his mom. But all this is useless. No matter how much it rots, there is no sign of it and there is still more than two weeks until the second competition.

## Chapter 5

*The day the purse was found*

One day, a very interesting thing happened in the life of Charlie and Alpha. No, I'm not lying, a very, very interesting incident happened. Now let's get to the point. One day, when Charlie and Alpha were looking for Mrs. Lilly, a man passed by them. At that time, a purse fell out of this man's back pocket. Isn't Charlie an honest person, pointing the purse at the person in front of him immediately:

"Hey, uncle, your purse fell," he said.

Then that uncle was very happy and took money from his purse. At that moment Charlie felt like a poor beggar. And he refused. But uncle lifted Charlie high and took him somewhere. Then he found out that this place is a big hotel. That uncle rummaged in his pocket and took out a key and pointed at Charlie:

- Thank you, child. I had more than a thousand dollars in this purse. I will be the director of this hotel. Now this room is for you! Yes, by the way, the gym is also yours to prepare for the second competition with your dog. Good luck - he said and left.

After that, everything changed. It seemed as if everything went ahead by itself. After all, didn't Charlie pitch a tent and sleep on the streets just yesterday? Now it is completely different. There is a warm room, a soft bed and even a large gym to train Alpha.

There are three days left for the second competition. Alpha is also well prepared.

## Chapter 6

### *The second competition*

The next day at lunch, Charlie and Alpha went to the second competition. As usual, they were greeted by Mr. Wright. Now Alpha and Alicia fight. I think Alpha is much braver than the previous ones and is no longer afraid of anything. There are so many people gathered in the big hall that if you throw a needle it won't hit the ground. As usual, when Mr. Wright finished his speech, the second competition started.
- Yes, Alpha, go ahead!!!
- Yes, go the wrestler puppy!!!
There are shouts and applause from everywhere. Even Charlie did not understand what happened. Yes, here's the thing, Alpha won. He left Alicia in the spot for jumping just one paw ago. Everyone except Alicia's owner is clapping in honor of Alpha. Even Mr. Wright is overjoyed. Screams are heard from all sides. Charlie does not stop jumping where he is. Alpha can't find a place to put himself. After all, isn't this a sign of luck? He arrived just a step away.
When they returned to the hotel, they were met by the director of the hotel, who had many gifts in his hand. He is also happy without himself. In general, it seems that everyone wants Alpha to win. Isn't it interesting that Charlie made a lot of friends before he came to this country. Yes, it is really very strange!
After entering the hotel room, they opened all their gifts one by one.
- Well, Alpha, it's the first gift. Ah, a wonderful bed for you! Well, well, here's the second gift, um, it's not a bad science-based book on dog language. And finally, the third gift is a lot of sweets for both of us! I think you like sweets, don't you Alpha? E-mmm, I think uncle has learned our taste. It seems that he really has a thousand dollars in his purse. Otherwise, he wouldn't have liked us so much.

Yes, now Charlie and Alpha's reputation has increased a lot. Now they are not just Charlie and Alpha, but "Charlie and Alpha". In the last week, only their picture was released. It's as if newspaper reporters have been sitting idle for a hundred years, and Alpha is the reason why they published his picture as if there was no other dog. But Alpha literally likes it. Even Charlie feels like the happiest person in the world. Of course, this is true. Who would have thought that luck would smile so much. Now Charlie and Alpha will not spend the night on the streets. They will not have to eat. That's why they say "Patience is golden". If Alpha passes the third condition, then the universe is beautiful. Look who you are, Corlin Charlie and his dog Corlin Alpha. But something still breaks the heart. Why hasn't the mom ever come looking for it? After all, how many magazines and newspapers appeared about him. Why is she not coming? It is even mentioned in every newspaper which hotel he is staying at. Maybe Charlie doesn't need his mother anymore. Maybe his mother is in another city and Charlie is in another city? But it hasn't been six months since he left. It's all a puzzle, use your mind and find it. What if Charlie comes so far and doesn't receive a letter saying "Are you okay, my son"? Very interesting. A person who is ready to give his life for his son is not interested in him now. It can't be like that, of course it won't happen. But the most important thing is not to deviate from the topic. Alpha should be prepared as much as possible. After all, he will be a rich dog soon.

To tell the truth, the above-mentioned uncle became a caring person for Charlie. He was with me on both bad days and good days. Alpha was also a great companion. But Charlie didn't tell his uncle about his mother. Uncle did not ask Charlie about his family even once. So it's not good to increase someone's anxiety - thought Charlie.

## Chapter 7

### *The third competition*

The next day, they went to the big hall where the third competition was held in front of everyone. Everyone arrived except Charlie and Alpha. When they came in, the big hall was filled with so much cheering and shouting that you could hardly stop. Everyone is cheering for Alpha. They even prepared a prize. I wonder how they did so much work. But the obstacles are so difficult that Charlie, seeing this, got stuck in his own spit. But for some reason Alpha is not afraid to be like flax. He believed in himself very much.

Well, let's move on to the area. In the test, almost all obstacles are made of fire. Only half of the obstacle at the end is fire and half is water. Until now, they had not put such a difficult test. Well, in any case, Alpha is not afraid. Is that not enough? If Charlie was in Alpha's place, he would have peed in front of these tests. Unfortunately, it's Alpha, not Charlie, who takes part in this challenge. What is this? Is this a spectacle shown in the circus, if they put so much fire on them?

- Sir Wright announced.

- Yes, Alpha will be. But some big ball is chasing after Alpha.

- What is this? Charlie asked Sir Wright.

- Haaaaaa, boom boy, this... this... accelerator!

- What an accelerator.

- If Mr. Alpha arrives without being caught by the accelerator, as I said before, two million is yours!

- If you can't come, how about putting an accelerator somewhere? What will happen then?

- Then? As I said before, this will be DISGRACEFULLY CHASED!!! Mr. Wright shouted suddenly.

- Why can't this happen, it's unfair!

- It doesn't matter, young man. Better watch the game while blessing your dog! That's the point. So?

At that moment, Charlie wanted to say, "Your hands are free," but held back his tongue.

- It's good - said Charlie, who couldn't find any other words.

- Here, a little more, yes, yes, yes, yes, dear Alpha is the winner. Oh, no, what happened? Charlie ran to Alpha. Oh my god, what happened? The accelerator hit Alfa's leg and broke it.

"But that doesn't count," declared Sir Wright with pleasure. Go out in front of people. I will give you your prize! "Don't be embarrassed," added Sir Wright in a whisper.

As Charlie forced himself to stand up, his thoughts remained on Alpha. After Mr. Wright ceremoniously handed over the money, Charlie took his leg in his hand and rushed towards Alpha.

- Where is Alpha? - Charlie quickly asked Mr. Wright.

- Alpha was taken to the hospital - answered Mr. Wright sharply.

- What hospital?

- If any dog is injured in this game, they will put me in the hospital on my behalf. Yes, they even go to the vet. That's what Mr. Corlin Charlie said. If I'm not mistaken, that's your name, right?

- Yes sir. Take me immediately to the hospital where Alpha is, or to the vet.

- Well, then get in the car.

- That's all, just hurry up please, sir.

- I said yes. You are impatient.

After at least ten minutes, they arrived at Alpha.

- How is the situation? Is the injury not serious?

- No, everything is fine. He just broke his leg. There is nothing else to say.

- Where is he now?

- In my room.

- Can I go and see?

- Why not, of course it will happen. Walk straight and turn left to room 31.

- Thank you.

- It's not worth it.

Charlie ran into the room. He was relieved to see Alpha. The injury is not as serious as the doctor and veterinarian said. Only his right leg is wrapped in bandages. But even seeing that, Charlie's heart was pulled back. Suddenly the vet came in. He loves dogs so much that he even talks to them like Charlie. Seeing that his dog was in good hands, Charlie's heart seemed to return to its place. The vet had a smaller piece of parchment in his hand as Charlie hadn't paid attention so far. As Charlie watched, the vet seemed to remember his dream, tentatively pushed a piece of parchment toward Charlie and said:

- This is a list of necessary medicines. "If you bring these things, your dog will soon be on his feet," he said.

Charlie ran towards the pharmacy with the parchment in hand. After getting all the necessary medicines, he returned to the vet. Veterinarian gave Alpha proper massage. But it was not allowed to take Alpha out of the church for three days. Despite this, Charlie sat in front of the Alpha and smiled. And finally, three days later, Alpha was allowed to be taken away. Charlie took Alpha for a walk one day. He brought ice cream, chocolate, and "dog food". So, Alpha was upset all day. Finally at 6:00 in the evening they entered their bedroom. They talked for a while and then started watching TV. The speaker's words are sometimes heard, sometimes not.

# Chapter 8

## *Looking for Mrs. Lily*

After walking like this for two or three days, they started looking for Mrs. Lily. Unfortunately, all this work went in vain. Mrs. Lily is nowhere to be found. Mrs. Lily was not found even after a week. Now how do they find a month? After all, they are looking for night as night and day as day. Is it possible that he has not watched television or magazines until now? Now, if anyone asks, he tells the address from memory. Something tugs at Charlie's heart. Even if he is - where will he find his mom now? After all, there is no place he hasn't seen, no hole he hasn't stuck his head in! When he asked Aunt Pippi, she said the name of the same town.

It is impossible to be mistaken. There's only one place left, but this cafe is now derelict. Well, just in case, you should check out that cafe. Charlie's hope was almost dashed, but because of that cafe, it seemed that a spark of hope gave him from the emptiness of his heart.

Charlie got up early the next morning, this time leaving Alpha at the hotel, and went to the unattended cafe. It is not necessary to hide that at first Charlie was afraid to enter this place without Alpha, but the inner voice did not stop calling him inside. His heart is pounding as if he will find his mom here, and he can't stay still. And finally, Charlie gathered all his energy and crossed the threshold. Although it looks like a ruin from above, it is not so scary inside. Charlie looked around. There is no danger here, but there is no his mom either. Charlie was trying to fix the pair from here in despair, when his foot tripped over something and fell into some kind of pipe. Since this pipe has been neglected for a long time, spiders have built a house on its walls. Charlie didn't even notice that he was standing on his feet because he was scared. Charlie's eyes continued to glow in the pipe until they adjusted to the darkness. After looking around, he noticed that there was a big door near the pipe. When he fell from the hill, his leg seemed to be stretched, he gathered all his strength and crawled towards the door. Charlie opened the door with fear, waiting for some unfortunate incident to happen. But no untoward incident happened. On the contrary, he entered the room where six statues were installed. All this seemed normal until the wall started to speak. Oh, he got lost, it was not the wall, it was the sound of a human being. There is no one in the room except Charlie. Then suddenly an old parchment fell into Charlie's hand. Charlie began to read the parchment:

*Hello my dear friend,*

*If you want to go to the main room,*

*You are asking our logic question.*

*Well, then read and listen to me.*

*Six statues will be given to you.*

*If you find a living person from here,*

*Then please open the door for you.*

*One of these is the living man,*

*The two are angels of death.*

*Another is a real statue,*

*Two of them are devil's females.*

*You find a real human race,*

*Hello, you are awake*

*The end.*

"Very interesting," Charlie wondered. I just need to find the human race here. Charlie walked slowly around all the statues. He heard the heartbeat of the entire statue. Only one statue has a heartbeat like Charlie's. Yes, this is a real human statue. Charlie touched the statue and immediately another piece of parchment flew out and landed in Charlie's hand. It contained the following sentences:

*Yes, you have found, my friend,*

*You are human.*

*The door is open to you.*

*Enter and blessings!*

—"It's great," said Charlie. And immediately he opened the front door and entered. Looking around, there were several women in this shop, including his mother.

- Oh, - shouted Charlie with joy.

- Charlie. You… you… What are you doing here? Oh my god, how did you know I was here? How did you pass the logic test? - Mrs. Lily became heated. And hugged Charlie. Now, go to where you are spending the night. Today is my last working day. Come to me at seven o'clock and we will go together. Good thing you're alive Charlie. Then Charlie left. He was surprised why he did not come here first. Charlie told the news and made Alpha happy. After that, both of them ate ice cream, watched TV and waited for 7:00 o'clock.

## Chapter 9

### *Happy days*

The clock is exactly half past six. Charlie took Alpha and set off. As it is almost dark, the outdoor part of some shops is illuminated by lantern light. They turned their direction towards the abandoned cafe, making sure that no one was watching. That place was also scary. It got dark and it became even more scary. The clock is still ten minutes ahead of the target. Now you have to wait ten minutes. Charlie blushed with joy. It was as if these ten minutes lasted for ten years. And finally it was exactly seven o'clock. But there is still no sign of Mrs. Lily. Charlie is now confused. Because his mother insisted on leaving work at seven o'clock. Suddenly he opened the door and entered. He walked the way he walked last time and appeared again in the same hole. He is not afraid anymore. He entered the room with the statue again. He did not even take the parchment and took the same path as before. He also found a human statue. Then he went inside. When he looked, his mother was lying in front of him. A letter is lying on it. The letter was covered in blood so much that if a little more blood flowed, the letters would become unreadable. The following sentences were written in the letter:

Anyone who finds out about our secret work will be executed. She was also killed so that your mother would not betray us because we killed you. After reading the letter, look back!!!

Charlie immediately looked back. However, he could only say a loud "Wow".

- No mom, Noo....

- Charlie, what happened to you? How are you? Are you feeling well?

- Hey, you...you...they executed you. I was just...hey...I was holding a letter in my hand. Yes... I see with my own eyes... me too...
- That's it, everything is fine. Today, I got off work at 7 o'clock... a little after 7:30 because I had a lot of work. When I came out, you were slumped over here in the old leather chair... I spent five minutes to wake you up. So, let's put an end to all this.

They were walking on the road in silence. But the dead silence was broken by Charlie's question:
- Hey, do you work in a secret department?
- What do you mean, my dear!
- Then why do you work in such a place?
- Because my boss kept it a secret so that others would not learn how we work.
- Then why did he ask a logical question?
- Because it will protect us from someone who looks at our wealth or attacks us. Wow, now you're only asking me questions, tell me about yourself, how did you get here?

Charlie told the whole story. During this time, they also arrived at Mrs. Lily's house. Mrs. Lily was surprised by these things. He also kissed Alpha.

"Oh, Charlie, have you been through so much?"

As soon as they entered the house, Mrs. Lily came to make coffee.
- Now we live here! Mrs. Lily exclaimed happily.

I haven't come out of the damn basement since I came here. now I work as a shop assistant.
- Great
- Yes, it's great
- I like it!

## Chapter 10

*The future*

So they became the happiest family. Days followed by months, and months followed by years. Charlie is considered the richest and kindest person in town. Because he created the safest sanctuaries for dogs and cats in the whole city. Hungry animals entered there and fed themselves. They buried Alpha's body in his yard and erected a two-meter statue on it. And he wrote a book about what he experienced in his whole life. It is said that it is impossible to read a book without crying. "If you don't strive for the future, there will be no future." Charlie sought the future and found his future. Even though they all left this world, they did not die. They will always be imprinted in our hearts with the good deeds they have done here and there, every honest work they have done!

***Norova Raykhona*** was born on June 16, 2010 in Uchkuduk District of Navoi region. Curruently, She is studying in a school in Tashkent. Her books were published under the name "Onajonim mehribonim" and "Porloq yulduz". She is the winner of various Republican competitions. Her articles were published in several local and national newspapers such as "Gulkhan", "Morning star", "Ma'rifat va ilm" and " Smile".

www.ingramcontent.com/pod-product-compliance
Lightning Source LLC
LaVergne TN
LVHW010418070526
838199LV00064B/5339